LIKE BUG JUICE

ON A BURGER

LIKE BUG JUICE ON A BURGER

BY JULIE STERNBERG

ILLUSTRATIONS BY MATTHEW CORDELL

Amulet Books, New York

The Library of Congress has catalogued the hardcover edition of this book as follows:

Sternberg, Julie.
Like bug juice on a burger / by Julie Sternberg ; illustrations by Matthew Cordell.
pages cm
Sequel to: Like pickle juice on a cookie.
Summary: "As the days go on, nine-year-old Eleanor realizes that maybe being at summer camp isn't so bad after all, and is full of special surprises" —Provided by publisher.
ISBN 978-1-4197-0190-0
[1. Novels in verse. 2. Camps—Fiction.] I. Cordell, Matthew, 1975– illustrator. II. Title.
PZ7.5.S74 Lf 2013
[Fic]—dc23
2012033169

ISBN for this edition: 978-1-4197-2049-9

Text copyright © 2013 Julie Sternberg
Illustrations copyright © 2013 Matthew Cordell
Book design by Melissa Arnst and Robyn Ng

Amulet Books and Amulet Paperbacks are registered trademarks of Harry N. Abrams, Inc.

Printed and bound in U.S.A.
10 9 8 7 6 5 4 3 2 1

Amulet Books are available at special discounts when purchased in quantity for premiums and promotions as well as fundraising or educational use. Special editions can also be created to specification. For details, contact specialsales@abramsbooks.com or the address below.

ABRAMS The Art of Books
115 West 18th Street, New York, NY 10011
abramsbooks.com

FOR ISABEL,

WHO HAS HAD HER OWN CAMP STRUGGLES,

AND FOR EMILY,

WHO WILL RUN THROUGH MUD

WEARING ONLY ONE BOOT

TO HELP ISABEL

—J. S.

I hate camp.

I just *hate* it.

I wish I didn't.

But I do.

Being here is worse than

bug juice on a burger.

Or homework on Thanksgiving.

Or water seeping into my shoes.

I want to go home right now.

I really do.

CHAPTER ONE

This all began one day
when Grandma Sadie called me up on the phone.
"I have a wonderful surprise!"
she said.
Right away,
the best possible surprise popped into my mind.
"You're giving us a dog?" I said.
Grandma Sadie was quiet.
Then she said,
"Eleanor, honey.
Your parents don't want a dog."
I knew that.
But I didn't understand it.
"We'd be so happy with a dog,"
I told Grandma Sadie.

"And I'm old enough to take care of it.

I'm nine."

"I know," she said.

"We could name it Antoine," I said.

"I love the name Antoine."

"Then I love it, too," she said.

"But

should we talk about your actual surprise?"

"Oh!" I said.

I'd almost forgotten about that.

"Sure."

"Well," Grandma Sadie said,

"I was just remembering

how much your mother enjoyed

sleepaway camp,

when she was a girl.

I think you'd also enjoy it.

So I'd like to treat you to sleepaway camp

this summer.

Would you like to go?"

"Yes!" I said. "I would!"

I really meant it, too.

"My friend Katie went last summer," I said.

"Every single day she ate M&M's.

And rode horses.

And jumped on a floating trampoline."

"How marvelous!" Grandma Sadie said.

"She got great at diving, too," I said.

"They gave her trophies."

"Let's get you started winning trophies,"
Grandma Sadie said.
"I'll call your mom's camp right away.
Camp Wallumwahpuck."
She did, too.
She called that camp with the crazy name
right away.

She also sent me a photograph, in the mail.
An old camp picture of my mom
when she was a girl.
She's standing outside a small white cabin,
wearing a backpack
and hugging a rolled-up, puffy sleeping bag.
She looks so happy.

I taped that picture to the wall by my bed
and looked at it night after night
before the start of summer.

All those nights,
I believed I'd be happy at Wallumwahpuck, too.
I really did.

5

CHAPTER TWO

The day before camp began,
my mom and I packed up together.
I read aloud from the camp list.
"'Two flashlights,'" I read, "'with batteries.'"
"One moment," my mom said.
She searched through shopping bags
and pulled out two flashlights
and two packs of batteries.
"Marker, please," she said.
I handed her a permanent marker,

and she started writing my name on a flashlight.

Because the camp list said to label *everything*.

"Next?" she said.

"'One sleeping bag,'" I read.

My mom pulled my sleeping bag into her lap.

It was so much thinner than hers had been.

I saw that without checking the photo

on the wall by my bed.

Because I already knew that picture by heart.

"Your sleeping bag must've been so much softer,"

I said to my mom.

"This one's plenty soft," she said,

writing my name on my bag.

"And remember what Natalie told us?

She has practically the same one!"

Natalie is my nice babysitter,

who has beautiful hair.

"I know," I said.

Natalie

"But I still like yours better."

"Mmm," my mom said.

She'd gotten distracted.

She sat very quietly for a second

with the bag in her lap,

thinking.

"What is it?" I asked her.

She smiled.

"I was just remembering how beautiful

Wallumwahpuck is," she said.

"You're going to have such a nice time."

Then she set my sleeping bag aside and said,

"What's next?"

"'Seven pairs of underwear,'" I read from the list.

"Get them, please," my mom said.

So I opened a dresser drawer

and started counting out underwear.

I gave my mom the stack,

and she uncapped her marker.

"Wait!" I cried.

She looked up, surprised.

"I don't want my name in my underwear!" I said.

"But what if you lose it?" my mom said.

"What if you drop it somewhere?

Like on your way back to your cabin,

after taking a shower."

"Then I *really* don't want my *name* in it!" I cried.

"I don't want everyone knowing

it's *my* dirty underwear!"

"Please, Eleanor," my mom said.

"Don't forget—

your laundry gets done after the first five days.

If you don't have your name in your underwear,

you won't get them back for the last five days."

"Oh," I said.

I tried to decide which was worse.

Everyone seeing my dirty underwear.

Or wearing *no* underwear for the last half of camp.

I couldn't decide.

Finally, my mom said,

"How about just your initials?"

"Fine," I said.

"But I'm leaving the oldest ones at home."

As she handed me back my most

worn-out underwear,

I realized

she wasn't going to be at camp with me at all.

Not even to help me put my things away.

Or make sure my flashlights worked.

Or tuck me in, under my thin sleeping bag.

My heart started to hurt.

"What if I miss you and Dad too much?"

I asked her.

"Will you come get me?"

"You won't miss us that much," she said.

"I can't even call you, can I?" I said.

I was starting to feel sweaty.

"Only in an emergency," my mom said.

"But what if they keep me from calling?"
I said.

"What if they're *evil*?"

I thought for another second.

"And what if they read my letters before
mailing them? To make sure
I'm not telling you their evil deeds?"

"I promise you, they're not evil," my mom said.

"The director was a counselor back in my day.
She's always been lovely."

I ignored that.

Then I had a brilliant idea.

"We'll have a code!" I said.

I came up with one, real quick.

"If I write in one of my letters,

'I just met Esmeralda,'

then you *must* rescue me.

Got it?"

"If you meet Esmeralda," my mom said,

"then I rescue you.

Can we finish packing now?"

"Yes," I said,

feeling much better.

"We can."

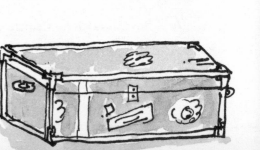

CHAPTER THREE

The next morning,
I stood with my parents
in a Brooklyn parking lot,
waiting for the bus to camp.
All around us,
girls were unloading cars
with their families.
A few of them had dogs, too.
Such lovable dogs,
wagging their tails and licking those girls' faces.

Sometimes girls would see one another across the lot
and scream

and run toward each other
and hug
and jump up and down.

I wanted a friend to run and hug and jump with.
I wanted my best friend, Pearl.
But Pearl goes to Oregon every summer
to visit her grandparents.

I also wanted a dog.

I frowned at my parents,
who kept crushing my dog dreams.
Neither of them noticed.
My mom was chatting with another mom.
And my dad had started walking off.
He stopped and talked to a woman with a clipboard.
She flipped through some papers,

then pointed across the parking lot.

Finally, my dad came back.

"Who was that?" I asked him.

"The head of the junior unit," he said.

"She says you're in the Gypsy Moth cabin."

"Gypsy Moth," I repeated.

"Isn't it pretty?" my mom said.

"I always wanted to be in
Gypsy Moth
when I was a girl."

"The *name* is pretty," I said.

"But aren't gypsy moths ugly?"

"They're prettier than *cicadas*,"
my mom said.

"I was in the Cicada cabin
my first year.

Do you want to hear how creepy
those bugs are?"

"No!" my dad said, very quickly.

My mom and I both laughed.

Because it's funny

how much my dad hates yucky things.

Then he told me,

"I have more news.

Your counselor is already at camp.

She'll meet you there.

But there's one other Gypsy Moth camper

getting on this bus.

Her name's Joplin."

"Really?" I said.

I'd never heard of anyone named Joplin.

"Really," my dad said.

"She's standing over—"

He turned to point,

then stopped and dropped his arm.

"That's her!" he said in a low voice.

"With the red glasses. Walking right toward us."

The girl with the red glasses
walking right toward us
was very thin
and very, very tall.
"She's *nine*?" I said.
She was as tall as a seventh grader!
"Yes, definitely," my dad said.
"I asked the same thing."
A second later,
Joplin stopped right in front of us.
My head barely reached
her shoulders.
We all said "Hi" and
"Nice to meet you."
Then Joplin looked down
at me and said,
"Do you eat chocolate?"
"Sure," I said.
I waited for her to offer me some.

Because why else would she have asked?

But instead, she said,

"Good.

A girl in my cabin last year said it gave her a rash.

I never liked her."

"Oh," I said.

We were all quiet for a second.

I wondered what that girl's rash looked like.

Then Joplin told me,

"Gypsy Moth is a good cabin.

It's near the bathroom.

So you won't get lost if you need to go

in the middle of the night."

"That's good," I said.

I started to imagine

being in my pajamas

lost in the deep, dark woods

with only a flashlight,

scared

and
searching for the bathroom
and
needing to pee.
Then someone called out,
"There it is!"
We all turned
and saw a big silver bus
with a sleek black top
pulling into the lot.
I stepped behind my mom when I saw it.
It was gigantic!
How was I supposed to get on that thing
without either of my parents?
"*You* have to drive me to camp!" I told them then.
"In our car!"
"You know we can't," my mom said.
"All campers arrive by bus—that's the rule."
"I hate that stupid rule," I said.

"We'll pick you up on your last day, though,"
my dad said.
"We can't wait to see you at camp!"
You'll have to wait *forever*,
I thought.
Because I am *not* getting on that bus.
I am *not*.
I'll stay *right here* in Brooklyn.
Maybe my dad read my mind.
Because he asked me and Joplin,
"Would you like to sit together on the bus?"
I held my breath.
Of course I wanted to sit with her.
But maybe she wanted to sit with someone else.
Or by herself.

She looked at me.

Sunlight bounced off her red glasses.

"Want to?" she asked.

"Sure," I answered.

Then the head of the junior unit shouted,

"Time to load up!"

"We'll meet you at the bus," my mom told Joplin,

"after you say good-bye to your parents."

"OK," Joplin said.

And she walked off

the way she'd come.

"Let's get this trunk on the bus," my dad said.

He took one end,
and my mom took the other.
I grabbed my backpack.
As we all crossed the lot toward the bus,
my heart started beating faster.
I hurried to catch up to my dad.
The trunk wobbled a little
as I took his hand.
I could tell it wasn't easy
for him to walk
holding the trunk with one hand
and me with the other.
But still,
he held my hand tight
until the very last second.
Then both my parents
hugged me
and kissed me

and reminded me to wear sunscreen and bug spray.
"Don't forget to reapply!" my mom said,
with her hands on my shoulders.
"It wears off!"
"I promise," I told her.
Suddenly, the head of the junior unit was shouting,
"All aboard!"
And Joplin was waiting beside me.
My mom kissed my head
one last time
before letting me go.
Then,
feeling very small,
I followed tall Joplin
onto the humongous bus.

CHAPTER FOUR

Joplin let me sit by the window.

"Thanks," I said.

She shrugged.

"I like to stick my feet out in the aisle," she said.

She stuck them right out there, too,

as soon as she could.

Other girls settled in around us.

The driver swished the door shut.

I looked out the window

and saw my parents.

They were standing beside each other,

shading their eyes with their hands,

searching the bus windows for me.

I waved and waved.

Finally, they saw me
and waved back.
Then the bus rolled past,
and they disappeared.
I turned—I didn't want to lose them.
But they were gone.

My body slid low in my seat.
And I thought,

Why am I going to this stupid camp?
Why did Grandma Sadie send me?
Why didn't I just say *no*?
"Are you going to vomit?" Joplin asked.
I thought for a second she could see inside me.
I thought she knew exactly how I was feeling.
But when I turned to her,
surprised,
I realized she wasn't talking to me at all.
She was looking at the girl across the aisle.
"Me?" that girl said, pointing at herself.
She had braces and two braids.
"Yes," Joplin said. "You."
"Why would I *vomit*?"
the braces girl said.
Joplin shrugged.
"Last year a girl got carsick
and vomited in the aisle.
I don't want vomit on my ankles."

Braces Girl made a face.

"That is *disgusting*," she said.

"I'm not going to vomit on your ankles."

"That's good," Joplin said.

Braces Girl turned away from us then

and said something to the girl sitting beside her,

and they both laughed.

I felt bad for Joplin.

Because they must have been laughing about her.

But Joplin didn't seem to care.

She just yawned.

And yawned again.

"My baby brother," she said to me.

"He has an ear infection.

He screamed all night.

I couldn't sleep."

"Oh," I said.

She closed her eyes and tilted her head.

"I need to rest for a second," she said.

And just like that,
she fell asleep.

I watched out my window for a while.
Rows of brownstones changed
to bigger buildings
with signs painted on their sides.

Like BEST HOT CHICKEN IN BROOKLYN.
We s-l-o-w-l-y crossed a long bridge
crowded with cars.
Then we inched through even more traffic until,
finally,
we were zooming up an open highway.
Buildings started disappearing
and trees started appearing
everywhere.
At some point,
Joplin's head fell on my shoulder
and stayed there,
bouncing a little with the bus.
No one had ever slept on my shoulder before.
Not even Pearl.
I thought about writing Pearl a letter,
telling her that my strange new friend
was bruising my shoulder.

But I couldn't get my stationery out of my backpack
without waking Joplin.
I kept watching out the window instead,
as the world outside
got greener and greener.

CHAPTER FIVE

Watching out that window

got boring.

So I slept, too.

Eventually, Joplin shook me awake.

"Look!" she said

when I'd opened my eyes.

She pointed out the window.

A sign there read:

WELCOME TO CAMP WALLUMWAHPUCK,

A HAVEN FOR GIRLS SINCE 1958.

The bus was bumping
down a gravel road
with bushes and trees and weeds all around.
This isn't beautiful,
I thought.
This is *creepy*.
I missed sidewalks full of people
checking their phones
and walking their cute dogs.
I missed paved roads, too,
filled with taxis and bike riders.
Finally, the bus turned
and stopped in a dirt lot.
"All right, girls!" the head of the junior unit shouted,
walking down the aisle.
"Step outside and find your counselors!"
"But we don't know who our counselors are,"
I said to Joplin.

"They'll be holding signs," she told me.

Sure enough,

when I stepped off the bus,

I saw teenagers holding signs:

GYPSY MOTH, DRAGONFLY, HONEYBEE, CICADA,

DOODLEBUG, MONARCH, PRAYING MANTIS,

HISSING COCKROACH.

"I'm glad we're not in Hissing Cockroach!"
I told Joplin.
"That one's fake,"
she said.
"The counselors make up a cabin name every year.
Last year it was Seed Head Weevil.
I still think they should use Seed Head Weevil
instead of Doodlebug.
Doodlebug is stupid."

I thought about that.
Doodlebug *was* babyish.
But still.
I wouldn't ever want to be
in Seed Head Weevil.

"Come on," Joplin said.
She started walking toward the Gypsy Moth sign.

I followed her.

We kicked up dust with every step.

And flattened weeds, too.

It seemed too quiet on that lot,

even with the sound of girls talking and laughing.

After a second,

I realized why:

no cars honking,

no sirens wailing,

no truck brakes squealing.

Just girls.

And a whole lot of birds,

chirping.

I didn't like it.

The Gypsy Moth counselor started waving

as soon as she realized we were walking toward her.

"Hello!"
she called.
"I'm Hope!"
She was wearing sunglasses
and red sneakers.
"I don't remember her from last year,"
Joplin muttered.
"She must be new."
"You're the Gypsy Moths
from Brooklyn!" Hope said
when we stood in front of her.
"So, one of you is Joplin,
and one is Eleanor."
We told her who was who.
"I am *so* excited to be
your counselor!"
she said, grinning.
She had a swinging ponytail

and freckles
and a pretty smile.
"I *love* Wallumwahpuck,"
she said.
"I was a camper here for seven years!
Then I spent a summer in Vietnam,
and last summer I went to Thailand.
Now I'm back!"

I looked around that dirty, weedy, too-quiet lot
and figured there must be a different,
more spectacular part of camp.
The part Hope and Mom both loved so much.

"Come on!" Hope said, smiling her pretty smile.
"Don't worry about your trunks;
someone will drive them over soon.
Let's get you both settled!"

CHAPTER SIX

The walk
to our cabin
was horrible.

Hope,
very bouncy and happy,
led us down a steep path
through tall trees
that let in small patches of light.
"We'll see the lake in a minute!" she said.
She moved fast down that path.
It was hard to keep up.
I had to wave swarms and swarms of gnats away, too.
They hovered in groups on the path,

not scared of me at all.

Like pigeons.

One even got on my tongue.

I was trying to pick it off

while I was hurrying to keep up with Hope,

so I wasn't paying attention

and I didn't see a tree root

that popped up out of the ground.

I tripped on it

and

flew.

When I finally landed,

skin had scraped off my hands

and my knees

and the bottom of my chin.

I just lay there,

sprawled on the ground

like dirty underwear.

And stinging all over.

"Eleanor!" Joplin shouted from behind me.

In a flash, Hope ran back up that steep path

and kneeled beside me.

"I'm so sorry!" she said.

"I was moving too fast!

I'm used to the roots now.

They're tricky, aren't they?

Everybody trips;
I don't want you to be embarrassed.
Come on up—
we'll take you right to the infirmary."
"No!" I said
as she helped me up.
I looked at my dirty red scrapes.
I didn't want to go the infirmary.
I wanted to go *home*.
I wanted my mom to sit me down in my bathroom
and wet one of our washcloths
with cold water
and dab it gently on my knees
and hands
and chin
until they were cool and clean.
Thinking about her—
I couldn't help it—

I started to cry.

"I'm fine," I said,

turning away from Joplin and Hope.

But I sniffled when I said it.

Hope reached to take my hands,

carefully,

and inspected the scrapes.

"It could've been worse,"

Joplin said.

"Last summer a Cicada fell out of a tree

and broke her leg.

She had to go home."

"Oh," I said,

still sniffling a little.

I didn't think I'd broken anything,

which was good.

But—to get to go home! How *lucky*!

"Can you walk?" Hope asked me.

"Yes," I said, wiping my face on my sleeve.

"There's a bathroom nearby,"

Hope said,

"with a first-aid kit.

Let's go clean you up.

Then, if we need to,

we'll take you to the nurse."

"OK," I said.

"We'll move very slowly," Hope said.

"Sounds good to me," Joplin said.

They both stayed beside me

as I limped down the path

ignoring the gnats

and avoiding the roots.

At the bottom

I saw a big, sparkling lake with wooden docks.

And,

off the end of one of the docks,

a floating trampoline.

I tried to imagine jumping
high and happy
on that trampoline.
But my knees screamed
when I thought about the landings.
So I ignored the trampoline, too.
And focused on the path beneath my feet.

CHAPTER SEVEN

After cleaning me up
and covering me in Band-Aids
and telling me not to worry about
the *three* scary spiders I saw
dangling and crawling around me,
Hope took us to our cabin.
It was small and painted white on the outside.
Just like my mom's, in her camp picture.
Do *not* think about that picture,
I told myself
very seriously.
Because it was too sad
to think about my happy mom.
I focused on Hope's red sneakers instead

as I followed her up the cabin steps.
Those red sneakers saved me
from crying *again*.

The screen door creaked when we opened it
and banged behind us when we got inside.
"Home sweet home!" Hope said.
It didn't look like home.
No rugs, no curtains, no lamps.
No couches, no armchairs, no tables.
No television, no stereo, no computer.
No colors on the walls.
Just brown wood, from floor to ceiling.
And four bunk beds, one in each corner.
And a few shelves and cubbies along the walls
under the windows.

Only my trunk was familiar.

It sat next to Joplin's, in the middle of the floor.
I wanted to curl up inside it.

"You both have top bunks!"
Hope said.
"Eleanor, you're there."
She pointed to a bunk bed on the left.
"And Joplin, that one's yours."
She pointed to the right.
Then she said,
"I have to meet our other campers.
Can you start unpacking without me?"
Joplin and I nodded,
and the screen door banged shut again
behind Hope.
Great,
I thought,
looking up at my bed.

Another way to fall.

My hands started burning again

just thinking about it.

Meanwhile,

Joplin had opened her trunk.

She was shoving clothes and towels

into the cubby by her bed.

I did the same thing.

Then she took out her sheets and sleeping bag

and stood on the edge of the bunk below hers

and started making her bed.

I tried to, too.

But I'd never made a top bunk before.

It was impossible.

Whenever I got one corner of the sheet

around that thin mattress,

the other corner popped off.

And I couldn't even reach the far side.

Finally, I climbed up on top
and crawled around
until I'd tucked everything in.
Then I climbed back down
and checked my bed
and saw
a disaster.
"Have bears been fighting up there?"

Joplin asked me.

I looked over at her bed.

It was *beautiful,*

smooth and tight.

Just like my mom's, at home.

"Don't worry about it," Joplin said.

"I got good at it last year.

Besides, it gets messed up anyway."

I knew that.

But still.

That bed was my only space in the whole cabin.

In the whole *world,*

until I got home.

I wanted to like it.

Joplin looked at my face.

"Hold on a sec," she said.

Then she stood on the bunk beneath mine

and, with her long arms,

pulled and reached and tucked
until my bed was beautiful, too.

My heart felt funny,
watching her be so nice.

"Thank you," I said
when she was done.
She shrugged.
"Don't tell anybody," she said.
Very serious.
"I don't want to be making everyone's bed."
"I won't," I said.
"I promise."

CHAPTER EIGHT

I pulled the Band-Aid off my chin
as soon as I heard the other girls
coming up the steps of our cabin.
Because that Band-Aid looked ridiculous.
It turned out all those other girls
were friends from the summer before.
Dylan, Montana, Kylie, Amelia, and Gwen.
"Look!" one of them said,
pointing out the window
as the rest were walking in.
"You can see our cabin from last year!"
"Where?" the others said.
They all leaned over my cubby
and knocked over my bottles of
sunscreen.

And talked over one another:

"Yes! I see it! There!"

"That was the *best* cabin."

"Didn't you *love* that cabin?"

I wanted to make them pick up my sunscreen.

Because that sunscreen

was important to my mom.

But I'd only just met them.

I didn't want to be bossy.

They probably wouldn't have heard me anyway.

They were still talking.

"Remember,"

one of them said,

"when Dylan was standing on that rock?"

And then

for some reason

they all started singing.

Something about a desperado

from the wild and woolly West.

"What's a desperado?" I asked Joplin.

"And why's the West woolly?"

She shrugged.

"Most of the songs here make no sense," she said.

That stupid woolly song was *catchy*.

I couldn't get it out of my head.

Even after those other girls stopped singing,

and Hope hurried us across camp for lunch.

CHAPTER NINE

We waited in a long line at the dining hall.

That line took forever.

I felt faint

from hunger

before I got to the food.

I longed for a juicy burger,

with ketchup only,

on a bun.

Just like my dad makes me, at home.

But when I finally got to the front of the line,

the teenager behind the counter said,

"Tuna?

Or meat loaf?"

I hate tuna *and* meat loaf.

I looked at both dishes.
One swimming in mayonnaise.
The other: hunks of gray meat.
"Do you have *anything* else?"
I asked the teenager.
"Salad," she said.
She pointed at a bin of lettuce
and tomatoes.
"And rolls."
I hate tomatoes, too.
But I said,
"I'll try a little salad.
And a lot of rolls."
"Two's the limit," she said,
dropping two rolls on my plate.
"Even if that's all I'm eating?"
I asked.
"Yep," she said.

She scooped me out some salad.
Then she looked at the person behind me
and said,
"Next."
My plate felt too light
as I walked to the Gypsy Moth table.
Joplin was already sitting there,
eating a huge tuna sandwich.
She stopped when she saw my plate.
"Aren't you hungrier than that?" she said.
"Yes," I said.
I sat down next to her.

"Would you please pass the bug juice?" she said.

I looked at her, confused.

She pointed to the jar beside me.

"That's *bug* juice?" I said.

"It's really just fruit punch," she said.

"Camp calls it bug juice."

I got an image in my head

of the blood and guts that gush out

when some bugs are squished.

"That's *disgusting*," I said,

handing her the jar.

She shrugged and said,

"It tastes fine."

But I was still disgusted.

I looked down at my plate.

Nothing looked good.

"When's snack?" I asked Joplin.

"I'll be so ready for M&M's."

"M&M's?"

She looked at me funny.

"There are no M&M's.

Wallumwahpuck is candy-free.

Always has been. It's a tradition."

"Candy-free?" I said.

It *couldn't* be.

I couldn't believe

I wasn't going to get

a single M&M.

My friend Katie's camp had given her *millions*!

"So what's for snack?" I asked.

"Frozen fruit bars," she said.

"And gluten-free cookies."

I dropped my fork on my plate.

This was even worse than my flying fall.

I've got to get out of here, I thought.

I really do.

CHAPTER TEN

After lunch and a camp tour

we all stood on the dock,

barefoot and in our swimsuits,

waiting for the swim test.

The wood was rough beneath my feet,

and the sun beat on my shoulders.

Straight through my sunscreen.

My stomach hurt, too.

And not just from hunger.

I'd never had a swim test before.

I didn't even swim very often.

My parents had made me take lessons,

and we'd gone together to the pool on weekends.

But it was always very crowded

with bigger, rougher kids

jumping and throwing things.

So we'd never stayed long.

Now,

as my face soaked up sun,

I worried.

"What if I fail the test?" I asked Joplin.

"Nobody fails," Joplin said.

"You get put in a baby group," Dylan said.

"Not a *baby* group," Joplin said.

"Just a group for beginners."

"Same thing," Dylan said.

What a *meanie*! I thought.

I wanted Joplin to lift one foot

and squash her.

A lifeguard in a red bikini blew her whistle then.

"Here's how the test goes," she said.

"Swim to the other dock and back

three times

without stopping.

Show me three different strokes."

She broke us into groups of two.

I swam last, with curly-haired Kylie.

We jumped into the deep lake together.

I kicked my way up for air, fast,

and gasped.

That water was freezing!

So much colder than the pool.

I could feel my lips turn blue.

The water was muddy, too,

which felt gross against my skin.

And I couldn't see a thing as I swam.

Plus, Kylie kicked me hard

when we were getting started.

I knew it was an accident.

But still.

It hurt.

Then,

doing the back crawl,

I bumped my head on the dock.

And,

doing the front crawl,

I forgot how to breathe.

Finally, I pulled myself out of the freezing lake

and back onto the dock.

I stood there shivering and dripping

as the lifeguard told us how we'd done.

Then it was official.

I was the worst swimmer in Gypsy Moth.

"You'll be in the Guppies swim class,"

she told me.

And only me.

Guppies were the second-lowest class,

next to Tadpoles.

A *baby* class.

Everyone else in my cabin was an Angel Fish

or a Shark

or a Great White Whale.

"She can't do breaststroke *at all*,"

I heard Dylan whisper to Kylie.

"She practically can't *swim* at all,"

Kylie whispered back.

I wanted to sneeze on their arms.

But I didn't have a sneeze in me.

I stepped away from them instead

and tried to hide in Joplin's long shadow.

The lifeguard still saw me, though.

"If Guppies want to go on the

floating trampoline,"

she told me,

"they need to wear a life jacket."

A life jacket! I thought.

That's like wearing a diaper!

Joplin turned to me.

"Life jackets aren't bad," she said.

"They're puffy."

I tried to smile a little,

because I knew she was being nice.

But it was hard to do.

We walked together off the dock.

Dirt stuck to the bottoms of my wet feet.

And,

when I reached for my towel,

I saw a mosquito on my arm,

sucking my blood.

I slapped it,

to kill it,

and it smushed into my skin.

I had to wipe the dead parts off with my hand

because I didn't have a tissue.

My poor hand.

Still scraped up at the bottom

and now smeared with bug parts

at the top.

CHAPTER ELEVEN

Hope gave each of us paper and pencil
that night at dinner.

"What's this for?" Joplin asked.

"A special project,"
Hope said.

"We have a baby goat in the barn.

We just adopted him from a local farm.

He needs a name.

So every camper gets to submit three choices.

The farm staff will vote for their favorite.

That'll be the name of the goat."

"Forever?" curly-haired Kylie said.

"Forever," Hope said.

We all sat down then.

The other girls started tapping their pencils

on the table.

Thinking.

Not me.

I knew the pet names I loved.

On my sheet of paper, I wrote:

1. Antoine
2. Sweet Pete
3. Cornelius

Antoine...   Sweet Pete...

Cornelius...

Then I folded that paper up.

Dylan was sitting next to me.

I sneaked a peek at her paper.

She wrote:

1. Bleat
2. Goatie
3. Spot

Good *grief*! I thought.

She can't name a goat *at all*!

Then I told myself

it was better to name goats well

than swim well.

I didn't really believe that.

But still.

I felt better.

After we'd all handed our lists to Hope,

we stood in the long line for food.

I had to eat salad and rolls again.

Because chili

is disgusting.

And the lasagna had spinach inside.

I asked for more salad this time

and forced myself to eat tomatoes.

Because I was *starving*.

CHAPTER TWELVE

Hours and hours later,
we were all wearing pajamas
and sitting in a circle on the cabin floor.
We all held our flashlights
shining up at the ceiling.

Hope set a candle in a dish
on the floor in front of her.
"Okay, Gypsy Moths," she said.
"As soon as I've lit this candle,
we'll all turn off our flashlights."
She lit the candle with a match,
and we all turned off our flashlights.
Now the flickering of one flame
was our only light.
It felt spooky.
But peaceful, too.
And I was so tired.
"We'll have candle lighting every night,"
Hope said.
"And we'll always start with a question.
Answer only if you want to."
She waited a moment.
Crickets chirped outside.

Then she said,

"Tonight's question is:

What was the highlight of your day?

Mine was meeting all of you."

We had a moment of quiet again.

Then Joplin said,

"Mine was the lemon-lime fruit bar."

And Dylan said,

"Mine was seeing Kylie."

And Montana said,

"*Hello?*

What about me?"

"You, too," Dylan said.

"And Amelia and Gwen."

Each of those girls then

talked about seeing the others.

I sat there, very quiet.

Thinking about my whole day.

I couldn't think of a single highlight.

After everyone else had finished,

Hope paused for a long moment.

Probably wishing I'd say something.

But I didn't.

So she stopped waiting

and taught us a song.

A much slower song

than the one about the desperado.

When we'd all sung together,

Hope blew out her candle.

As we switched on our flashlights, she said,

"One more reminder before bed.

You must never bring food into the cabin.

It attracts animals."

"Like rats!" Amelia said.

"Rats?" I said.

"That's right!" Kylie said.

"We had one in our cabin last year.

Because of *Dylan*."
I had to shake my foot then.
I could practically feel a rat on it.
"My mom sent cake," Dylan said.
"It was delicious."
"That rat thought so, too!" Kylie said.
"Okay," Hope said.
"If she sends cake this year,
we'll store it safely in the dining hall.

Now, everyone into bed."
So I climbed into bed.
It was strange, being so high.
And the mattress was lumpy,
and my sleeping bag was thinner and more slippery
than the quilt I used at home.
And my parents weren't there
to tuck me in
and kiss me good-night.
But I barely thought about any of that.

81

Because before most of the girls had turned off
their flashlights,
I had fallen asleep.

CHAPTER THIRTEEN

In the middle of the night, I had a nightmare.

About a rat

hanging on to the leg of my jeans,

tight,

with its pointy teeth.

I shook

and shook

my leg,

trying to fling it off.

I tried so hard,

I woke myself up.

Then I sat up,

confused.

I was relieved
there was no rat.
But I didn't know where I was.
Just that I wasn't home.
Nothing felt like home.
Not even the air.

When I heard the crickets outside,
I remembered.
And I lay back down.
I wanted to call out for my mom.
She'd bring me a glass of water
and rub my back
and say, "It was just a dream.
Don't worry.
It was just a dream."
I couldn't believe
I hadn't made it through a single night yet.

I couldn't believe

I had nine more to go.

I remembered my whole rotten day.

My flying fall.

My stinging hands

and knees

and chin.

This stupid, lumpy bed,

which I couldn't even make.

The swim test.

The mosquitoes.

The no-candy rule.

The rat.

The spiders spinning in the bathrooms

every time I went to pee.

Changing my clothes

in front of girls I barely knew

before swimming

and after swimming

and again before bed.

I don't want to be here,

I thought.

I hate camp.

I just *hate* it.

I made an important decision then.

I fumbled in the dark for my flashlight

hanging on the wooden frame of my bed.

Then,

very quietly,

I climbed down my bunk ladder.

Gwen was breathing

a slow, whistly kind of breathing

in the bunk below mine.

I tiptoed past her

and got stationery and a pen from my cubby,

then climbed back up the ladder

and started writing a letter.

I wrote:

Dear Mom and Dad,

I have met Esmeralda.

Remember, Mom?

I have met Esmeralda.

I can't wait to see you both.

This is how much I miss you:

You are still the best parents in the world.

And there's no better grandma than Grandma Sadie,

who was trying to give me a present.

I still love you from the tips of my toes

to the top of my head

and out into the sky.

Even though you sent me here

with no warning at all

about the candy

or the bug juice

or the spiders

or the life jackets.

All my love,

Eleanor

I sealed that letter in an envelope
and addressed it.
As I was pressing on the stamp,
I heard a noise behind me.

I turned quickly,

scared.

But it was just Hope.

She stood at the foot of my bed and

rubbed her eyes.

"Everything okay?" she asked me.

"Yes," I said. "Thanks."

Then I handed her my letter.

"Would you mail this for me?

In the morning?"

I asked.

"Of course," she said. "First thing."

My whole body felt lighter then.

I knew I'd be going home soon.

I switched off my flashlight

and fell right back to sleep.

CHAPTER FOURTEEN

We chose our own activities the next morning.

Joplin chose tetherball.

So I chose tetherball, too.

Even though I'd never heard of it.

And I decided to try to have fun.

Since this would be one of my last days at camp.

We walked together to a field

with poles scattered around it.

Each pole had a ball attached,

hanging from a rope.

When activity time started,

a counselor explained the game.

"Each pole will have two of you,"

she said.

"You are opponents.

If your opponent hits the ball one way,

you hit it back, in the opposite direction.

Don't let her hit the ball so many times that

the rope wraps all the way around the pole.

Whoever wraps the rope all the way around

wins.

Got it?"

She waited, to see if there were questions.

There weren't.

It didn't seem too hard.

"Let's give it a shot," the counselor said.

So Joplin and I walked to a pole,

to give it a shot.

"You start," I said,

being very nice.

She took the ball

and raised it high

and *hurled* it.

It flew in a circle

far, far above my head.

Then sailed back her way,

and she hit it,

hard.

This happened again and again.

So high and so fast,

I never even touched the ball.

It took about five seconds

for her to wrap the rope all the way around the pole.

After she did, she grinned at me.

"Isn't tetherball *great*?" she said.

"No, it is *not*," I said.

But I couldn't help laughing a little.

Because that game had been ridiculous.

Then I turned and shouted,

"I need a shorter opponent!"

I ended up playing a short Honeybee.

I even won two games

and lost two more.

Joplin won six straight
against a tall,
but not tall enough,
Cicada.

CHAPTER FIFTEEN

I wanted to spend time with the baby goat.

So I chose farm as my next activity.

I asked Joplin if she wanted to come, too.

But she shook her head.

"The barn's too stinky," she said.

I knew what she meant.

We'd visited the barn on the camp tour,

and it *was* a little stinky.

But just with animal smell.

Like at the zoo.

"Your nose gets used to it," I told Joplin.

"My nose would rather play soccer," she said.

So we walked together to the soccer field.

She stayed there, to play.

And I kept going.

The barn stood, wide and white,

at the other end of the field.

It was dark and cool inside,

and a little stinky.

A few girls had arrived before me.

They were peering into a wire cage in a back corner

and saying things like,

"*So* cute!" and

"So *fuzzy*!" and

"Look at its little *wings*!"

I knew little chicks were hopping around in that cage.

I'd seen them during the camp tour.

They *were* cute and fuzzy,

with tiny little wings.

But still.

I preferred the floppy-eared goat.

He was lying in the back of his pen,

on top of some hay.

Just thinking.

When I stopped in front of his gate,
he sniffed the air a little,
then pulled himself up and walked toward me.
He was brown from head to toe,
the color of my dad's morning coffee.
"They'd better not name you Spot," I told that goat.
"You don't have a single spot on you."
He pushed his nose through a gap in the gate.
I scratched underneath his chin
and kept thinking about names.
He didn't seem like an Antoine.
Maybe a Sweet Pete.
But definitely,
definitely
a Cornelius.
"Don't you think so?"
I asked him,
patting his back.

"Don't you think you're a Cornelius?"
He gave a nice bleat.
I took that for a yes.
I couldn't keep talking to him, though.
Because other girls arrived
and stood beside me at the gate.
Including curly-haired Kylie.
Before long,
the farm counselor told us it was time
for the goat's bath.
We went into the pen
and wet him gently with a hose
and rubbed baby shampoo into his soft coat
and rinsed him off.
He did not like the rinsing!
He jumped around
and shook his whole body,
splattering water all over us.

Then the counselor looped a leash over his head

and let me walk him out into the sun,

so he could dry.

As I led clean Cornelius out onto the grass,

I thought,

I'm walking a goat!

He wasn't a dog.

But still.

For that moment,

I could pretend

he was mine.

CHAPTER SIXTEEN

For lunch we had a choice
of black beans with yellow rice
or sloppy joes.
I don't like beans of any color.
And I hate orange, oozing sloppy joes.
"Can't we ever have burgers?"
I asked the lunch teenager.
"Sloppy joes are like burgers," she said.
"No, they are *not*," I said.
"They are nothing like burgers."
She shrugged
and heaped even more salad than usual on my plate.
And I ate lettuce and tomatoes with lots of croutons
for lunch.

I'd never known before

that croutons are *delicious*.

I ate three rolls, too,

instead of just two.

Because Joplin gave me one of hers.

CHAPTER SEVENTEEN

I worried and worried during rest hour,
after lunch.
Because swim lessons were next.
I'd have to go to my baby class
and then make my way to the floating trampoline
wearing my diaper.
I lay on my bed, worrying.
I'd just decided to fake
a stomachache
when Hope walked to the
middle of the cabin floor.
"Mail time!" she said.
She looked at the first letter
in her stack
and called Dylan's name.

Then,

looking at the next letter,

she called mine!

"Your very first letter at camp!" Hope said,

handing me my letter.

"Thank you!" I said.

I ripped that letter right open

and started reading.

I read:

Dear Eleanor,

I want you to receive a letter every single day.

So I'm writing to you already,

even though you *just* left on the bus.

The apartment feels so empty without you.

I put on the radio, hoping it would fill the space a little.

But it doesn't work!

By the time you get this,
you'll have spent at least a day and a night at camp.
I so hope that you're happy!
Some of my very best memories from childhood
are from Wallumwahpuck.

It might be a little hard for you in the beginning,
being away from home for the first time.
But I know how strong you are.
And how capable you are.
And I'm certain that in the end
you'll have wonderful memories, too.
I'm so pleased about our new family tradition!

Your dad will write you soon.
He's at the grocery store now,

because we're out of coffee.

You know how he loves his coffee!

But not nearly as much as we both love you.

Please don't forget to write us!

We can't wait to hear from you!

All my love,

which is a TREMENDOUS amount of love,

Mom

I read that letter twice,

then set it on my bed.

I didn't have to fake a stomachache anymore.

My stomach really did hurt.

Because I'd ruined our new family tradition

by hating camp.

I wasn't strong and capable, either.

I'd already sent the Esmeralda letter.

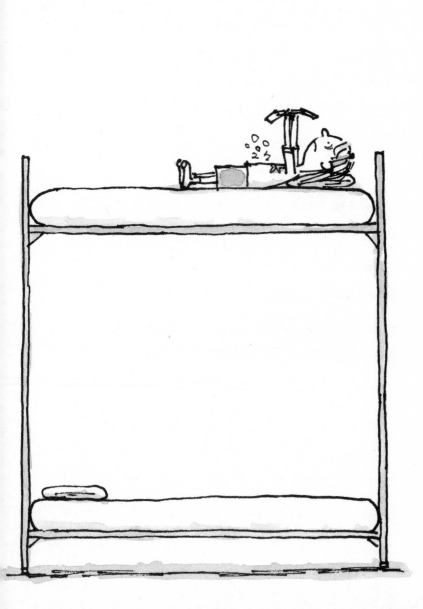

And I still wanted to leave.

I wanted to be home.

Not lying on this thin, lumpy mattress

so close to the cobwebs

drooping from the ceiling.

I tried to figure out

whether to write my mom again.

And what to say to her if I did.

But before I could,

Hope told us to put on our bathing suits.

Because it was time for swimming.

CHAPTER EIGHTEEN

At least I wasn't the oldest Guppy.

Braces Girl from the bus

was a Guppy, too.

I was pretty sure she was older than me.

Because of the braces.

I couldn't tell if she recognized me from the bus,

because she kept looking down at the dock

while we all waited for the Guppy teacher.

After a few minutes that teacher arrived

and blew her whistle.

"Everybody in the water!"

she said.

Braces Girl was the first one in.

I jumped in second.

That water was still freezing!

But I warmed up

because our teacher made us swim forever!

Five laps of backstroke,

then five of freestyle.

She must have liked my backstroke fine.

Because she never said anything about it.

But after one lap of freestyle,

she tapped me on the head.

I held on to the dock, kicking my feet,

and looked up at her.

"Watch,"

she said.

She showed me how to breathe,

two or three times,

then sent me off again.

"Show me a stronger kick," she told me

after the third lap.

I tried hard for the rest of the laps,

kicking and breathing.

"Better," she said

when I was done.

"Much better."

I'd never swum ten laps before

in my whole life.

I figured our lesson *must* be done.

But when the last of the Guppies returned

to the dock,

our teacher said,

"I want everyone to tread water now

for five minutes.

Or until you can't tread anymore.

Ready? Set!

Go!"

I wasn't sure I could tread at all.

My legs were tired!

But I moved away from the dock,

not far from Braces Girl,

and I started to tread.

After about a minute,

I was facing away from the dock,

struggling to keep my head above water,

when I heard my name.

I kicked around.

Joplin was standing on the dock,

dripping wet.

She waved at me.

I did *not* wave back.

I knew if I did,

I'd sink to the bottom

of the lake

and never rise

again.

"You're moving your legs too much!"

she shouted.

"Slow down!"

"Shut up!" I wanted to shout back at her.

But I could barely breathe.

"Move less!" Joplin shouted again.

"Pedal a bike slowly!"

Actually,

I realized,

moving less sounded good.

So I stopped kicking fast

and started pretending to pedal a bike slowly.

It *was* easier.

Much easier.

Joplin kept shouting directions at me.

And when our teacher blew her whistle

after five minutes,

I was still treading.

CHAPTER NINETEEN

I didn't want to go
on the floating trampoline.
"I'm tired," I said.
I *was* tired.
Swim lessons had just ended.
"Sorry," Hope said.
"It's a cabin activity.
Go and get your life jacket."
So I had to go all by myself
to the swim shack, next to the dock.
It stank of mildew in that shack.
The floor was covered with paddles and ropes.
And life jackets hung crookedly
on rods.

They came in all different sizes.

I had to guess at mine.

The first one I picked was filthy,

so I put it back.

The second one was filthy, too,

and it had a broken clasp.

These things are ancient! I thought.

Then I realized something.

My mom might have stood in that very spot

and flipped through those very life jackets

when she was a camper.

In a funny way, in that moment, I felt her beside me.

Which made me happy.

But only for a second,

because then Joplin stuck her head through

the shack's door.

"Ready?" she said.

"Everybody's waiting."

I grabbed the next life jacket I saw

and threw it on.

Even though it was enormous.

Then Joplin and I ran together to the dock.

Hope frowned at my giant life jacket.

But she just said,

"OK, everybody!

To the trampoline!"

The rest of the cabin leaped right into the water

and started *racing* to the trampoline.

I jumped in last.

I could tell it was going to take me *forever*

to kick my way to the trampoline.

Because my stupid life jacket kept dragging me back.

Hope stayed beside me the whole time,

doing an easy breaststroke in her striped bikini.

"I wish I'd had that life jacket last summer,"

she said.

"Swimming in the ocean, in Thailand."

"What *happened*?" I asked.

I figured it must've been scary and awful.

Since she'd needed a life jacket.

But she said,

"My bikini top fell down!

I hadn't tied it tight enough!

I needed a life jacket

to keep me covered!"

I laughed.

"It was *horrible*!"

she said,

laughing, too.

"I had to tread water

practically naked,

until I finally got my top back on."

"I don't even own a bikini,"

I told her.

"So a life jacket doesn't help *me*."
"You can borrow one of mine!"
Hope said.
I laughed again.
Because the thought of me
in one of Hope's bikinis
was just ridiculous.

Something about Hope's story
made me feel better.
Even though all the other girls
were already jumping on the trampoline,
and I was still the only one in a puffy diaper.

"Listen up, everybody," Hope said,
after I'd followed her onto the trampoline.
"Sit in one big circle.
We'll jump two at a time."

I didn't want to jump at all.

I just wanted to be invisible.

But when it was Joplin's turn,

she pulled me by the hand.

"Come on!" she said.

"Jump with me!"

We bounced together.

Lightly at first,

then harder and harder.

Until we knew exactly when to

STOMP

to make each other soar.

CHAPTER TWENTY

After candle lighting that night,
I fell asleep to the sound of raindrops on the roof.
But I heard no rain when I woke up
in the middle of the night.
Instead,
I heard
a tapping.
On the window above my cubby.
It stopped after a few seconds.
Then started again.
I knew—
I just knew—
there was a man out there.
Making his way inside.

"Hope!" I tried to say.

I could barely get a sound out.

The man tapped again.

I closed my eyes and tried harder.

"Hope!"

She came then,

so fast.

She shined her flashlight all around

and saw that I was the only one awake.

"What happened?" she whispered to me.

"There's someone out there!" I said.

"Someone's trying to come in!"

I pointed at the window.

"I don't think so," she whispered,

shining her flashlight in that direction.

We couldn't see anything in the beam of light

except my bottles of sunscreen.

Hope walked over and peered out

for a good long time.
Then she came back to me.

"It's just a branch," she whispered.
"Knocking against the windowpane
in the wind.
I promise—there's no one there."

I tried to relax.
But I couldn't.
What if he'd just hidden behind a tree?

"I'm still scared!" I whispered.

She thought for a second.

Then she walked back over to my cubby,
picked up a bottle of sunscreen,
and brought it back to me.

It was such a weird thing to do.
Why would I possibly need sunscreen?
It was the middle of the night!

But I took the bottle from her.

123

"No one's out there,"
she whispered.
"But just in case,
use this.
Spray him right in the eyes.
And call me.
I'll take care of him. OK?"
"OK," I said.
I set the sunscreen next to my flashlight.
Then she tiptoed back to her bed.
And
after listening carefully
and hearing no more tapping
and telling myself again and again
there's no one there,
I finally fell back to sleep.

CHAPTER
TWENTY—ONE

At lunch the next day,

someone tapped me on the shoulder.

I turned

and almost fell off my chair.

It was the *camp director*!

"Are you finished eating?" she asked.

I nodded,

speechless.

I'd never seen her talk to a camper before.

She made announcements

and drove around in a golf cart

and spoke into a walkie-talkie.

Why did she care if I'd eaten?

"I'm taking Eleanor for a second,"

the director called across the table to Hope.

I looked with wide eyes at Joplin.

She looked with wide eyes back.

"Come," the director said to me.

My brain raced as I followed her.

But I couldn't think of why she wanted me.

She led me into a little office

and shut the door behind us.

We sat down at a round table.

I waited for her to speak.

"I just received a call,"

she said.

"From two very worried parents."

"Oh,"

I said.

I looked down at the table.

I knew she meant *my* parents.

I knew they must've read my Esmeralda letter.

"This happens every year," she said,

sounding very kind.

"Someone has a tough start to camp.

I've thought about your situation,

and I've come up with a plan."

I looked at her serious face.

"Have you heard about the Wall of Feelings?"

she asked.

I nodded.

Hope had told us about it.

Every summer,

girls write down their feelings about camp

and post them on the dining hall wall.

For everyone to see.

"We're starting the Wall of Feelings tomorrow,"
the director told me.
"I want you to post two pieces there.
One about how you felt
when you wrote that letter home.
And one about how you feel now.
Be absolutely honest, please.
You do *not* need to include your name.
Lots of people don't.
But you do have to be honest.
And include pictures!
I've heard you're a good artist.
After that,
if you still want to go home,
you come and tell me.
I'll give it *serious* consideration.
How does that sound?"

I thought for a second.

Something worried me.

"If I write honestly about my feelings,"

I said,

"I'll say bad things."

"Of course!" she said

with a big smile.

"That's perfect!

Who wants a Wall of Feelings that only says

'I love camp,'

'I love camp'?

That's boring!

Besides, happiness is only one feeling.

It's a Wall of *Feelings*.

Plural.

So you have an important role to play.

Can you do it?"

I nodded.

"Good," she said.

"Don't forget.

If you still want to go home,

you let me know.

OK?"

"OK," I said.

She stood up.

I stood up, too.

"One last thing," she said.

"Will you please write your parents

a little something positive?

To make them feel better?"

I nodded again.

Then she opened the door and set me free.

CHAPTER
TWENTY-TWO

I sat in my bed at rest time
and thought and thought and thought.
Of positive things.
Then I wrote a letter to my parents.

I wrote:

Dear Mom and Dad,
My counselor is nice.
I got to walk a goat.
And gluten-free cookies are okay,
as long they're chocolate chip.

Here is a picture of me walking a goat.

And here is a picture of a gluten-free cookie.

All my love,

which is the MOST POSSIBLE love,

Eleanor

When I finished,

I handed my positive letter to Hope.

"Will you please mail this? *Soon?*"

I said. "It's important."

"I will,"

she said.

"I promise."

CHAPTER TWENTY-THREE

I had farm that afternoon.

It was nice to see Cornelius.

But he had a big sign on his pen

that said:

OUR GOAT'S NAME IS

ALFIE!

CONGRATULATIONS

TO JACKIE BOBROW,

PRAYING MANTIS

I felt like tearing up that sign.

Alfie was a stupid name!

Cornelius was so much better!

I bent down

and looked that goat in the eye.

"Do *you* like Alfie?"

I asked.

He gave a little snort.

"Me neither," I said.

Soon after that,

the farm counselor gathered all the kids in the barn

and taught us how to clean the pens.

"Yuck," Kylie kept saying

as we shoveled out Cornelius's stall.

It *was* pretty yucky.

But I figured

Cornelius couldn't clean his stall himself.

And he deserved a nice space.

So I didn't mind.

CHAPTER
TWENTY-FOUR

I took a fast shower after farm.
Then,
still wearing my bathrobe,
and with my hair still dripping wet,
I sat on my bed
and chewed on a pen
and tried to think.
Because I had to write my two pieces
for the Wall of Feelings.
The camp director had told me to describe
how I'd felt about camp
the night of the Esmeralda letter.
And how I felt about it now.

I squeezed my eyes shut
and recalled the Esmeralda night,
when I'd just skinned my hands and knees and chin
and failed my swim test
and then woken, terrified, from a rat nightmare—
in the middle of the night, in a strange room
and a strange bed,
with no chance of seeing my parents.

I could remember *exactly*
how that felt.
So I opened my eyes
and started writing.

I wrote:

I *hate* camp.
I just *hate* it.

I wish I didn't.

But I do.

Being here is worse than

bug juice on a burger.

Or homework on Thanksgiving.

Or water seeping into my shoes.

I want to go home right now.

I really do.

I drew a picture next.

Because the camp director

had told me to.

I'd just finished when Joplin rushed over,

startling me.

"Come *on!*" she said.

"Dinner starts in three minutes!"

I gasped

and leaped off my bed
and threw on some clothes.
Because of this camp rule:
Any camper late for a meal
must sing a crazy song about a chigger
to the whole dining hall.
We'd already seen one poor Cicada do it,
and two Dragonflies,
at breakfast that morning.

After I'd pulled on my shoes,
Joplin and I both sprinted from our cabin.
She was cheetah-fast,
with her ridiculously long legs.
I huffed and puffed behind her,
thinking,
I will *not* sing that chigger song
all by myself.

I will *not*.

I pushed myself harder than I ever had before.

And reached the dining hall,

sweaty and exhausted,

five seconds behind Joplin.

And just barely in time.

CHAPTER TWENTY-FIVE

Hope let me skip flag-raising the next morning.
Because I still hadn't even begun to write
my second piece for the Wall of Feelings.
It was so quiet as I sat on our cabin steps,
with no one else around.
Just me and a couple of birds
in the trees around me,
chirping at each other.
I hugged my knees
and thought and thought
about all that had happened
since the Esmeralda night.

Then I wrote:

I hate swim lessons.

But I like being better at treading.

I hate not having my thick quilt.

But I'm getting used to my bed.

I don't like tetherball with tall people.

But I do with short.

I like Cornelius a lot.

I just wish he wasn't named Alfie.

I hate chili and sloppy joes and bug juice

(and the chigger song).

But croutons

are delicious.

I miss my parents.

But I like my counselor and my very tall friend.

And,

more than anything else,

I hate my stupid life jacket.

When I'd finished writing, I added this picture:

Then I went to find Hope.

So I could give her my pages to post.

CHAPTER
TWENTY—SIX

I visited the Wall of Feelings that afternoon
and read other girls' pieces.
Which were so *enthusiastic*.
"Camp Wallumwahpuck rocks!"
a lot of them said.
And
"I *never* want this summer to end!"
"I *love* this place!"
"Camp Wallumwahpuck is *heaven*!"

Why can't *I* love camp?
I thought,
reading all of that.

I was glad I hadn't signed my name
on my own negative pages.
I hoped no one could tell they were mine.

I kept reading and reading
until finally
I found one other piece
that was negative, too.

It said:

"I don't care what everyone says—
I don't love this camp.
But I don't need to love it.
I just need to survive it."

I read that piece
again and again.
And started feeling better.

I wished that girl had signed *her* name.

I wished I could meet her.

I don't need to love this place,

I told myself,

walking away from the wall.

I just need to *survive* it.

I can do *that*.

Only,

I might have to start stealing rolls.

CHAPTER
TWENTY—SEVEN

Camp went by faster after that.
I saw the director sometimes, on her golf cart.
She always waved at me,
and I always waved back.
But I never asked to go home.
Not even after I got a bug bite on my eyelid,
and my eye swelled half-shut.

I quit some activities because
of that bug bite.
Like archery.

Because it's dangerous to shoot a bow and arrow

with one eye swollen half-shut.

I still had to go to swim lessons, though.

And,

after our seventh lesson,

our teacher tested us

to see who could move on, beyond Guppy.

I worked so hard during that test

to breathe just right

and show my teacher a strong kick.

I was determined, too,

to tread water the longest.

And I did it!

I pedaled a bike very slowly,

just like Joplin had taught me,

and outlasted all the other Guppies.

Only by six seconds.

But still.

I did it!

"Congratulations," my teacher said to me

after I'd swum back to the dock.

"You are officially an Angel Fish."

My whole cabin was hovering

when she said that.

Because I'd told Joplin about the test,

and she'd told everyone else.

They all jumped up and down

and cheered for me.

Then Hope shouted,

"To the trampoline!

No life jacket

for anyone!"

We all ran and leaped into the water together.
I loved sinking
deep, deep underwater
and kicking my way to the top.
Instead of bobbing on the surface like a duck,
in my diaper.
Then I raced with everyone else through the water
to the trampoline ladder.
I wasn't the first to arrive.
But I wasn't the last, either.
And that felt good, too.

As soon as I'd climbed up,
Joplin grabbed my hand.
And we
STOMPED
for each other again; and we
SOARED,
first one, then the other, again,

high into the sky.

Later,

after changing into dry clothes,

I had an idea.

I explained it to Joplin,

and she said she'd help.

We gathered what we needed

and went outside.

I slipped my backpack onto my shoulders

and hugged my thin sleeping bag

and stood in front of my small, white cabin.

The way my mom had stood in front of hers,

so long ago.

I smiled,

thinking about my surprisingly nice day.

And Joplin took my picture.

I knew I wouldn't look as happy as my mom did

in her picture.

I knew she really loved Camp Wallumwahpuck

and thought it was beautiful
and had never written an Esmeralda letter.
I knew she'd probably had a million happy days
at camp.
Still,
I liked having one
of my own.

CHAPTER TWENTY-EIGHT

On the very last morning of camp,
Joplin took a pen
and wrote her Brooklyn phone number on my hand.
"You have to come over,"
she said.
"My apartment is not candy-free."
I wrote my number on her hand, too.
And we promised to visit.

Soon after that, my parents arrived.
Right away,
my dad threw his arms around me

and lifted me in a big hug,

right off the ground.

"Oh, how you've grown!" he said,

setting me down.

I couldn't stop smiling.

My mom hugged me, too,

and looked at me close.

"So gorgeous!" she said.

"How long have you been this gorgeous?"

"Forever," I said.

We both laughed then.

Because that was just ridiculous.

And because we were happy.

Both of my parents thanked Hope

for taking care of me.

She smiled her pretty smile and said,

"It was my absolute pleasure."

Then my dad said to me,

"We're not leaving
until your mom and I meet your goat."
So I walked them to the barn.

When we passed the tetherball poles, my mom said,
"I used to love that game!"
"Let's play!" I said.
I reminded her of the rules,
and we played a long, fun game
that she eventually won.
Because even though I'd grown,
she's still a lot taller.

After that we kept walking.
We passed Braces Girl
and the teenager who often served me lunch.
They both waved.
And the teenager called to me,

"Good-bye, Salad Girl!"

"Who's Salad Girl?" my mom asked.

"I am," I said.

"I eat a lot of salad."

"You *do*?" she said.

"Do you like pickles now, too?" my dad asked.

"Definitely not," I said.

"And by the way,

will you make me a juicy burger when we get home?

With ketchup only,

on a bun?"

"Of course I will!" he said. "I'd like nothing better."

We'd arrived at the barn then.

"It's exactly the way I remember it," my mom said.

"Even the smell!"

Inside,

the farm counselor was feeding the animals.

"Eleanor!" she said
when she saw me.
"We're really going to miss you."
"I'll miss you, too,"
I said.
"Your daughter is so helpful with the animals,"
she told my parents.

"You see?" I said to them.

"I'm a huge help with animals.

And dogs are animals!

So can we get one?

Please?"

My parents looked at each other.

"We'll see," my mom said.

And my heart went flying.

Because I could tell,

I could just tell,

that she really meant

yes.

CHAPTER
TWENTY-NINE

Grandma Sadie called me up on the phone

about a week after I got home.

"I just received a very nice thank-you note," she said,

"from a very nice granddaughter."

"That's me!" I said.

And then I had to say,

"Can you hold on a second, please?"

Because my little puppy,

Antoine,

Antoine

was trying hard to climb into my lap.

His wagging tail almost knocked over

the new double picture frame on our coffee table,

with my mom's camp picture on the left
and mine just beside her on the right.

"Careful!" I said,

lifting him up.

He licked my face,

and I set him on my lap.

"Sorry about that,"

I told Grandma Sadie.

"I'm back now."

"I hear there's a new member of the family,"

she said.

"And that you're taking good care of him."

"I'm bad about feeding him from the table,"

I said.

I had to laugh,

because he was climbing all over me.

"Otherwise, I'm very good."

"He must have been a wonderful surprise,"

Grandma Sadie said.

"But I gather camp wasn't?"
I almost said, "That's true."
But I caught myself
and thought for a minute instead.

I thought of soaring through the air with Joplin,
and Cornelius's brown eyes.
I thought of delicious croutons
and tetherball.
I thought of treading water the longest
and taking a camp picture of my very own.

And then I said,
"Sometimes—
not always,
but definitely sometimes—
camp *was* a wonderful surprise."

Here's a sneak peek of Eleanor's next adventure in *Like Carrot Juice on a Cupcake.*

LIKE CARROT JUICE ON A CUPCAKE

I did a mean thing.

A very mean thing.

To a new girl AND

to my best friend.

I HATE that I did it.

But I did.

This is worse than

carrot juice on a cupcake

or a wasp on my pillow

or a dress that's too tight at the neck.

I hope you never do anything that mean.

I really do.

CHAPTER ONE

It all started one Monday morning in April
when our fourth-grade teacher,
Mrs. Ramji,
made a special announcement.
She was standing near her desk,
beside a girl I'd never seen before.
That girl wore sparkly clothes
and a headband with a big bow.
"We have a new student!" Mrs. Ramji said.
"This is Ainsley Biggs.
She just moved here, from Orlando!"
"Orlando!" my best friend, Pearl, whispered to me,
from the desk beside mine.
"How *magical.*"
I heard other kids whisper, "Disney!"

And then the boy who sits behind me,

Nicholas Rigby,

started humming the Disney song

"It's a Small World."

He hummed and hummed,

just loud enough for me to hear.

"Shh!" I told him.

I turned and glared at him, too.

Because Nicholas Rigby is always

getting us in trouble.

Plus, I knew I'd never get that song out of my head.

"Doesn't Ainsley look like a present?"

Pearl whispered to me.

"A shiny present, too pretty to unwrap?"

(Pearl talks like a poet sometimes.)

"She *does* look like a present!" I whispered back.

I started wondering

whether *I* ever wanted to look like a present.

Before I could decide,

Mrs. Ramji turned the lights off

and on again

to get our attention.

"Class 4A!" she said.

"Please settle down!

You're not behaving your best for Ainsley.

We need to make her feel welcome!

It's not easy,

starting a new school so late in the year."

Then Mrs. Ramji said,

"Pearl!"

Pearl sat up straighter,

and I did, too.

Because maybe she was in trouble.

But Mrs. Ramji told Pearl,

"I would like you to move your desk

closer to Eleanor's, please."

"*Closer* to Eleanor's?" Pearl asked.

"Yes," Mrs. Ramji said.
"Actually, everyone in that row,
move a little
to make space for Ainsley's desk,
on the other side of Pearl."
"Yay! Closer to you!"
Pearl whispered to me,
and we grinned at each other
as everyone in our row
started making space for Ainsley.
After we'd finished
and I'd sat back down,
a wadded-up ball of paper flew
through the air
and landed on my desk.
I knew exactly
what that flying paper was.
I opened it up
and smoothed it out.

Sure enough, Nicholas Rigby had drawn me a picture.

This one showed me on a roller coaster

in Orlando,

with my arms in the air

and my hair blowing in crazy directions.

I folded the picture neatly

and put it on top of the pile

of Nicholas's pictures

that I kept in my desk.

Because even though that boy's impossible,

he's still a ridiculously good drawer.

Then I turned and whispered to him,

"Thanks."

Like I always did.

And he kicked the back of my chair,

not too hard,

like *he* always did.

Then Mrs. Ramji asked us

to take out our Creative Writing notebooks

and work on our Brooklyn Bridge poems

while she and Pearl helped Ainsley get set up.

I loved my Brooklyn Bridge poem.

So I worked on it very hard.

And realized only later

that I should've been

paying attention to Ainsley instead.

Because during that time,

she started casting a glittery spell over Pearl.

She really did.

ABOUT THE AUTHOR

Julie Sternberg is the author of *Like Pickle Juice on a Cookie* and *Like Carrot Juice on a Cupcake*, which tell more of Eleanor's stories. Formerly a public interest lawyer, Julie is a graduate of The New School's MFA program in writing for children. Like Eleanor, she hates pickles and pickle juice, bug juice, sloppy joes, and meat loaf. Also like Eleanor, she is particularly fond of M&M's. She lives in Brooklyn, New York.

ABOUT THE ILLUSTRATOR

Matthew Cordell is the author and illustrator of *Wish* and the illustrator of *Like Pickle Juice on a Cookie*, *Like Carrot Juice on a Cupcake*, and many more books for children. He lives in a suburb of Chicago.